Dingo Dog bared his teeth.

He **howled** until the sand whipped up.
"What are you doing at **MY** billabong?"

He **growled** until the ground shook.
"How dare you drink **MY** water?"

Dingo Dog

and the Billabong Storm

Andrew Fusek Peters   illustrated by Anna Wadham

Dingo Dog was feeling ever so thirsty.
He padded his way down to the billabong for a nice, cool drink.

And who was there do you think, sipping and slurping
all his precious water?

Kookaburra, Goanna Lizard, Kangaroo, Snake and Desert Mouse!

When Kookaburra, Goanna Lizard, Kangaroo, Snake
and Desert Mouse saw Dingo Dog with his **SHARP** claws,
charging towards them, they ran for their lives and hid in the bush.

Later that day, they gathered in the shade of a macadamia tree.

"Dingo's a **BULLY!**"
said Kookaburra.

"I agree!" wailed Kangaroo.

"What shall we do?" said Snake.

"Find another billabong!"
suggested Goanna Lizard.

"No!" squeaked Desert Mouse,
"I have a much better idea..."

The next morning, the sky was blue
and Dingo lazed in the shade of the tree.
He was daydreaming about a nice swim
when suddenly he heard a noise nearby.

"**Hmmm!**" he hissed.
"Whoever's woken me up
is going to be in **BIG TROUBLE!**"

Dingo looked up into the branches of the tree and saw Desert Mouse
and all her family scurrying round and screeching in a panic.

Dingo Dog was furious.

"What a racket you're making!
Can't an old dog find any peace?
How about I crunch you up
for a little bit of breakfast?"

The mice ignored him.
Each of them had a rope,
and they were tying
themselves to the branches.
"Quick! Quick!
We don't have much time!"

"Time for what?" asked Dingo.
"Have you gone mad?"

Desert Mouse looked down at the dog.
"Dear Dingo, we're not mad, but wise. Don't you know,
the **GREAT BILLABONG STORM** is on the way? We're tying
ourselves to the tree, otherwise the wind will soon blow us all away!"

"Don't be ridiculous!" said Dingo. "The sky is blue and the sun is hot.
There's no storm out there, little mice with even littler brains!"

Two of the mice dropped some macadamia nuts on Dingo's head.

"**OW!** What was that?" Dingo wailed.

"The first hailstones!" squeaked Desert Mouse. "Oh my, it's going
to be a **BIG STORM!** Sorry, Dingo, there's no time to talk."

Dingo frowned. The sky was blue, the sun was hot. It didn't make sense!

Far away in the bush, the kangaroo began slapping
his tail on the ground, until the earth began to **SHAKE!**

"Here comes the **THUNDER!**" squeaked the mice.

Dingo's eyes **rolled around,** looking for the storm.

Now, Kookaburra began **scratching** and **tapping** the tree trunk with her beak.

"Here comes the **LIGHTNING!**" squeaked the mice.

Dingo cowered, expecting the sky to fall on his head
He was in **DANGER!** What could he do?

He looked up at the mice.

"Give me your ropes!"
he snarled,
"or I will **EAT YOU**,
bite by bite!"

"If you insist!" said the mice.

They dropped the ropes
right by his paws.

Dingo tried to tie himself to the tree.
But his paws were useless.
By now his teeth were **chattering**
and **clattering** with fear.

"Get down here little mice,
and **TIE ME UP!**"

"If you insist!" sang the mice.

They climbed down the trunk and tied
Dingo Dog in knots, squealing all the while:
"The **BILLABONG STORM** is coming!
The **BILLABONG STORM** is coming!"

Kookaburra tapped **HARDER!**

Kangaroo thumped his tail **LOUDER!**

The mice threw **MORE** and **MORE** nuts!

Dingo trembled all over.

"And while you're about it, tie them good and tight!"

"If you insist!" sang the mice.

Snake slithered into the water
and swam around fast, making huge ripples.

Goanna Lizard burrowed beneath the ground,
throwing up fountains of sand, as if the wind had already arrived.

Dingo shook! Dingo shivered!
Dingo shouted! "TIE ME TIGHTER!"

The mice ran around, until Dingo
was done up like a parcel.
At last he felt safe and secure.

"HO! STORM!
Come and do your best!
I'm not frightened of YOOOOU!
You can take the mice and
carry away the other animals,
but you can't touch me!"

All of a sudden, the sounds stopped dead
and a silence fell.

The sky was blue and the sun was hot.

Kookaburra, Desert Mouse, Kangaroo,
Snake and Goanna Lizard all came out of hiding
and surrounded Dingo Dog.

"What's going on?"
Dingo demanded.

"Oh **SILLY, STUPID** Dingo!" laughed Kookaburra.

"Look at the sky! It's blue!" Snake hissed.

"Just like we felt blue when you stole the billabong!" said Goanna Lizard.

"The storm didn't get you, but we did!" said Kangaroo.

"We'll let you go, as long as you promise never to use
this billabong again! You could have shared the water with us,
but greed turned you into a **FOOL!**" added Desert Mouse.

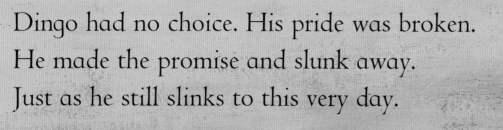

Dingo had no choice. His pride was broken.
He made the promise and slunk away.
Just as he still slinks to this very day.

The sky was blue and the sun was hot.
And Kookaburra, Kangaroo, Snake,
Goanna Lizard and Desert Mouse sat round
their **BILLABONG**, having a nice, long, cool drink.